THE NAUGHTIEST GIRL
HELPS A FRIEND

The Further Adventures of Enid Blyton's
Naughtiest Girl

The Naughtiest Girl Helps A Friend

Anne Digby

*Hodder
Children's
Books*

a division of Hodder Headline Limited

First published in Great Britain in 1999
by Hodder Children's Books
This edition published in 2005
For sale in the Indian Sub-continent only

10 9 8 7 6 5 4 3 2

For further information of Enid Blyton,
Please contact www.blyton.com

A Catalogue record for this book is available from
the British Library

ISBN 0 340 91094 1

Typeset by Avon Dataset Ltd, Bidford-on-Avon, Warks

Printed and bound in India by
Gopsons Papers Ltd., Noida

Hodder Children's Books
a division of Hodder Headline Limited
338 Euston Road
London NW1 3BH

Contents

Contents

1 A big responsibility for Joan

'Look, Joan!' exclaimed Elizabeth, as they emerged from behind the stables. 'Look at all the tents! The teachers and the seniors must have put them up for us. There were only bushes and trees and grass and buttercups here this morning. Oh, Joan, I do hope Miss Ranger will let me be in your tent. I'm so proud you've been made a tent monitor!'

The two friends paused, out of breath. Their kitbags, stuffed full of spare clothes and camping equipment, were heavy. They each carried a pillow and a sleeping bag, too. They were making their way from the school buildings across to the camp site.

Putting everything down for a moment, they leaned against the stable wall and gazed at the scene beyond.

'To think that's where we'll live for the next few days!' laughed Elizabeth, clapping her hands. 'Oh, won't it be fun? I'm so glad neither of us is going home for half term. Isn't it just like a little secret village?'

For all children staying on at Whyteleafe School over half term, a summer camp had been organised in the school grounds. And this wild corner, beyond the stables, made a perfect camp site. The school tents had been brought out of storage. They were ex-army bell tents. Supported by a central pole, their roofs tapered to a point and they were high enough to stand up in. The tents were dotted along both banks of an old dried-up stream bed. On a washing line, strung between two willow trees, some bright tea-towels billowed gently in the sunshine.

'Why, yes, it does look half like a village,' Joan agreed, quietly. 'The brown tents are like little houses. Except they haven't got any windows in them, of course,' she added. She touched the large torch that was sticking out of the top of her kitbag.

'At least this torch will be useful at night when it gets dark inside.' All the tent monitors had been told to bring a torch – only one was allowed per tent.

That reminded Elizabeth.

'I'll *die* if I haven't been put in your tent!' she repeated. 'I begged and begged Miss Ranger to say I could be. I wonder what she's decided?'

'Hadn't we better go and find out?' asked Joan, with her gentle smile.

'Yes, let's!'

The two friends humped their kitbags over their shoulders once more. With their pillows and sleeping bags rolled under their arms, they staggered onwards. The ground was uneven here, with large tussocks of grass to step round. But they went as fast as they could. Elizabeth was beginning to feel tense now. Joan, too, looked rather anxious. What would Miss Ranger have decided?

Elizabeth and Joan were best friends. At one time they had been in the first form together. In those days Elizabeth had been called the Naughtiest Girl in the School and Joan had been her only true friend. Joan was older than Elizabeth and had gone up into the second form some time ago. In fact, she was a second-form monitor. It meant that the friends saw far less of each other in term time than they used to. It was going to be marvellous fun being at camp together, thought Elizabeth, and even better if she could be in Joan's tent.

Miss Ranger, Elizabeth's form teacher, was to be in charge of the girls at camp, assisted by Rita, the head-girl. The boys, whose tents were pitched on the other side of the dried-up stream, would be answerable to Mr Leslie, the science master, and William, the school's head-boy.

'You will sleep four girls to a tent,' Miss Ranger had explained to some of them. 'There will be a school monitor, or one of the senior girls, in every tent. She will be known as Tent Monitor. She will be responsible for the happiness and wellbeing of everyone in her tent. As there will be a little junior girl to look after in most of the tents, it will be an important responsibility.'

The boys' side of the camp would be run on similar lines.

'Will we still have Meetings, so we can air our Complaints and Grumbles?' Arabella Buckley had asked, eagerly. She would have loved to have been a tent monitor herself, able to boss people around. But as there was no hope of that, she was uneasy. 'I mean, if there are any problems that the tent monitor can't solve?'

'Oh, yes, there will be the usual Meetings, with William and Rita in charge,' Miss Ranger had assured her. 'But they will be held in the open-air. I hope you can keep them nice and short.'

And now, as the two friends reached the camp site, here was Miss Ranger coming to greet them.

'Hello, Elizabeth. Hello, Joan. You are almost the last to arrive! My goodness, you're certainly heavily-laden, Elizabeth. Here, let me take your pillow and sleeping bag.'

'It's my fault we've taken so long, Miss Ranger,' confessed Elizabeth. 'I couldn't decide which books to bring, or whether to bring my yo-yo, and then I couldn't get everything into my kitbag—'

'Never mind!' replied the first form teacher. 'Follow me.'

She led them past the nearest tents and through to a large clearing. Here the ground was level. Ground sheets had been spread out, with bags and bedding piled high. Lots of girls were milling around Rita, the head-girl. Rita was holding a list and directing the girls to their various tents. Beyond, a brick barbecue had been built and a fire lit. The delicious smell of toasted muffins mingled with woodsmoke drifted towards Elizabeth. Beyond the barbecue, a camp kitchen had been set up. In fact, it was still being built. Thomas, a senior boy, was banging some stakes into the ground with a mallet, while Mr Leslie sawed some rough planks.

The two friends dumped their things on a ground sheet and gazed round at all the activity with interest.

'This is Camp Centre!' explained Miss Ranger. 'It's a very busy place, as you can see.'

Elizabeth stared across at the list in Rita's hand.

'Please, Miss Ranger, will I be in Joan's tent?' she blurted out.

'Yes, indeed, Elizabeth,' replied the teacher, lightly. 'I've decided that Joan will be the best person to keep you in order.'

The friends exchanged joyful looks.

'Oh, I'm so pleased,' said Joan, quietly. She rarely showed emotions but the relief on her face was unmistakeable. 'I'm sure Elizabeth will be a great help to me.'

'Joan will *not* have to keep me in order, Miss Ranger!' said Elizabeth. Even though the teacher had made the remark lightly, it had stung just a little. She was *not* the Naughtiest Girl any more. She was going to be as good as good could be.

'Of course not,' replied the teacher. 'Joan, may I have a quiet word with you, please? It's just about your junior.'

As the teacher took Joan to one side,

Elizabeth went and stood by the kitbags and gazed about her. She was in a happy little dream. She was definitely going in Joan's tent! Life was perfect. It was a sunny day and they had been promised more good weather to come. The sky was completely blue. And how fine the big bell tents looked! Much better than those low ones that you had to crawl into. It would be like living in their own little house!

Which tent would they be given? And which of the younger girls were they being asked to look after? Miss Ranger had warned them there would be a junior in most of the tents.

'Elizabeth!'

Joan walked across and joined her. The teacher had departed.

'Miss Ranger has told me where our tent is. She says we can just pick up our things and go straight there. You see,' she explained, 'it seems that Teeny's been here quite a while. She's sitting in the tent, waiting to get to know me.'

'Teeny Wilson? Is that who we've got?' asked Elizabeth cheerfully. Noticing that her friend looked rather pale, she added: 'What's the matter, Joan? Teeny won't be any trouble for you to look after. I'm sure she couldn't say boo to a goose!'

Tina Wilson was new at Whyteleafe School this term and small for her age. She was the smallest member of the junior class, which was why everybody called her Teeny. Elizabeth had noticed the timid little girl standing alone at playtime, her spectacles too big for her small, round face.

Miss Ranger had confided to Joan that Teeny was not settling down well at her new school. She seemed rather shy and nervy. She would no doubt find sleeping in a tent rather strange at first, even a little scary. The teacher had reasoned that calm, gentle Joan was exactly the reassuring presence at camp that Teeny needed. She had told Joan as much.

'It's going to be a big responsibility, looking after Teeny,' was all Joan would say.

'No, it isn't. It's going to be fun!' replied Elizabeth, as they headed along the bank towards the last group of tents. 'We'll make sure she has a good time. Am I going to be a big responsibility, too?' she teased her friend. 'I promise I'll be good. You know I'm not the Naughtiest Girl in the School these days!'

Joan barely smiled.

'Ssh,' she said. 'That's our tent at the end. She mustn't hear us talking about her. And, wait Elizabeth, there's something else I have to tell you. Let's put our things down a minute.'

Obediently Elizabeth propped her things against a willow tree but she was hardly listening.

'What, Joan?' she asked, staring impatiently towards the brown bell tent that was to be their home for the next few days. The flap was partly open. She was longing to peep inside, see what it was like in there, and make friends with Teeny. She and Joan would soon put the little junior at her ease. 'What a glorious position!' she exclaimed. 'We're right in the corner.'

The tent was pitched by the school's high boundary wall. The crumbling old wall's dark red brickwork was almost hidden in places by cascading honeysuckle. Elizabeth could smell the sweet scent, wafting on the warm breeze, even at this distance. By the wall, the bank of the old stream dropped down to where the dried-up water course came to an end at a culvert. The culvert, an old brick-built tunnel, would once have carried the flowing water underground for a short distance. Now the stream bed was just dry, powdery dust and the entrance to the culvert choked with rubble and weeds.

'It's about the other person in our tent,' Joan was saying. 'It's going to be Arabella.'

'Arabella Buckley?'

As Joan's words sunk in, Elizabeth groaned.

'Oh, no, not Arabella!'

Then she suddenly giggled. She was too happy today to let anything dismay her for long. She thought of her rich, spoilt classmate, with her pretty doll-like face. Arabella was always perfectly groomed and thought a great deal of herself.

'Miss High-and-Mighty at camp!' she exclaimed. 'Having to slum it in my tent. Oh, Joan, this should be funny!'

'Now, promise me you two won't quarrel—' began her friend.

'Don't be so tent-monitorish!' laughed Elizabeth. 'It depends how badly Arabella behaves whether we quarrel or not. Come on, Joan, what are we waiting for? Let's go and investigate the tent right now! As long as Arabella doesn't do anything silly and make me lose my temper, there's nothing to fret about!'

She grabbed Joan's hand and bounded towards the last tent.

She was far too excited to notice the frown on her friend's face or to hear her soft reply.

'Knowing Arabella, I'm worried she might.'

And that was not the only thing that Joan was worried about.

2   *Arabella accuses Elizabeth*

As the face peered in at her, the tiny, bespectacled girl in the tent gave a nervous start.

'Peep-o! Hello, Teeny!' cried Elizabeth boisterously.

Then she ducked into the tent, followed by Joan.

The small child shrank back into the shadows, just inside the tent. Her hands were shaking a little.

'Oh, I'm sorry,' she apologised. 'You made me jump.'

Teeny was on her own. Arabella had gone off somewhere.

'Isn't it lovely in here?' said Elizabeth, as her eyes got used to the gloom. She danced round the tall, stout tent pole in the centre. 'Look, Joan! You can stand straight and walk around in the middle! Isn't this fun?'

'I've put my things over there,' Teeny was telling Joan, shyly. She pointed to the far side of the tent. 'It's nice and dark and cosy over there. Is that all right, Joan? Am I allowed?'

Joan at once gave permission.

'What a good idea, Teeny,' said Elizabeth. 'I think I'd like to sleep that side, too. Unless you want to, Joan?'

'Oh, no, I'll be quite happy here,' said Joan sweetly. She was crawling around near the open tent flap, in the very small space that Arabella had left clear. 'I like to be near the fresh air!'

'Arabella's taken up far too much room though,' Elizabeth pointed out. Arabella's sleeping bag was already fully unrolled, with her personal belongings piled all around. 'She's been in and unpacked, then, Teeny?'

'She was here very early,' replied the junior. 'She wanted to bag a good place in the tent, she said. She's gone to get a muffin now. Please, may I go and get one, as well, Joan?'

'Of course, Teeny,' replied Joan, gently. 'Off you go. And while you're out, Elizabeth and I will bring our stuff in and sort it out.'

'We'll get the tent ship-shape!' added Elizabeth, eyeing Arabella's things. There was a glint in her eye. Did Arabella really think she was going to get away with having twice as much space as the rest of them? Not if Elizabeth could help it!

The two friends went outside to collect their belongings. They watched the figure of Teeny hurrying off through the tents, looking this way and that as she went.

'What a jumpy little thing!' observed

Elizabeth. 'But she really likes you, Joan. I can tell that already. She really looks up to you.'

'I do believe she does,' agreed Joan.

When the two friends had finished sorting things out, they sat outside the tent in the sunshine to take a rest. It was then that Arabella appeared.

'I've had to move a few of your things, Arabella,' Joan said pleasantly. 'You hadn't left me quite enough room. And would you mind rolling your sleeping bag up, please?'

'Whatever for?' asked the fair-haired girl. 'I've arranged it just how I want it for bedtime tonight.'

'Because it's a camp rule,' replied Joan, quietly. 'Kitbags must be kept packed during daytime and sleeping bags rolled up. With four people using the tent during the day, we have to leave enough space for people to be able to move around.'

'Oh, sorry. I didn't know,' replied Arabella. 'Though I can't think who will want to spend time in the tent during the day, when it's so sunny outside. I certainly won't.'

Giving Elizabeth a rather pointed stare, she ducked into the tent to attend to her sleeping bag. Elizabeth smiled to herself. *What good news*, she thought.

'Come on, Elizabeth,' said Joan, rising to her feet. 'If we're going to the village, we'd better stroll down there now. I've got my purse.'

'Are you sure we've got time?' asked Elizabeth. Reluctantly, she, too, got to her feet. 'We could always go tomorrow.'

'I've looked at the rota. We've got plenty of time!' replied Joan. 'We're down for Kitchen Duties at six o'clock and that's two whole hours away.'

Joan had discovered that her torch batteries were getting low. She wanted to

go to the village and buy some spare ones.
It was a strict rule at Whyteleafe School
that if pupils wished to walk down to the
shops during free time, they must always
go in pairs. Naturally, Elizabeth had agreed
to accompany Joan. But in truth she would
have much preferred to spend the free time
exploring the camp site. There was so
much jollity and excitement going on.
There was going to be a barbecue round
the camp fire that evening!

'If you say so—' began Elizabeth.

And then suddenly there came a loud
screech from inside the tent.

A moment later, Arabella burst out,
hurling her sleeping bag on the ground in
front of her.

'What have you put in my sleeping bag,
Elizabeth Allen?' she shrieked. 'Take it all
out, whatever it is. If you put it in, you can
take it out! I suppose I was meant to feel
all that stuff in the dark, when I climbed

into my sleeping bag at bedtime!'

'How dare you!' exclaimed Elizabeth, in amazement. Her own voice rose in anger. 'Whatever are you talking about? How dare you start screaming at me!'

Girls from nearby tents were now peering out, to see what the rumpus was about.

Arabella turned to Joan, for support.

'When I started to roll my sleeping bag up, it felt all lumpy!' she screeched. 'Then I put my hand inside and there was something all wet and yukky. And there was something prickly, as well. Feel inside, if you don't believe me!' Her voice rose to a high-pitched squeak. 'I'm sure anybody in the *world* would scream at Elizabeth, if she did the same thing to them!'

As Joan bent down to unzip the sleeping bag, Elizabeth could feel herself starting to boil with rage.

She hardly cared what Joan was pulling

out of the sleeping bag. A wet sponge, Arabella's hairbrush, a bar of sticky soap, a little nailbrush . . .

'Oh, dear. Poor Arabella,' Joan was saying, rather helplessly. 'Somebody's been playing a joke on you . . .'

Elizabeth was too busy fighting to control her hot temper. Then—

Arabella walked up to Elizabeth!

'I suppose you think it's funny? I suppose you were really looking forward to watching me get into bed tonight—'

She gave Elizabeth a hard push.

And at that point Elizabeth boiled over.

'Why should I want to bother to play a joke on you, you stupid creature!' she shouted. 'Everybody knows you've got no sense of humour. I don't know anything about your silly sleeping-bag—'

'Fibber!'

'I expect you did it yourself to get me into trouble!'

'Fibber! Fibber! Fibber!' shrilled Arabella.

'Don't you dare call me a fibber!'

Elizabeth made a lunge at Arabella while Joan stood there, looking aghast, just as the next-door tent monitor came racing over.

'*Stop it*!' she cried. It was Philippa, one of the senior girls. 'Who's the tent monitor around here? Can't they keep order?'

It was the sight of Joan's ashen face that calmed Elizabeth down. She took a step backwards. Arabella, too, backed away.

'That's better,' nodded Philippa. 'If you've got a disagreement, just learn to settle it in a civilised way.'

She returned to her tent.

Then a tiny figure tip-toed out from behind the nearby willow tree. It was Teeny Wilson.

She looked very white and trembly.

She walked straight up to Arabella.

'Please don't blame, Elizabeth,' she said. Her voice was barely more than a whisper. 'It wasn't her who played the joke on you.'

Arabella looked startled.

'Who was it, then?' she asked.

'It was me,' said Teeny.

They all gasped. Then Teeny turned to Elizabeth, miserably.

'It was only going to be a – a bit of fun. I didn't mean somebody else to get the blame.'

Elizabeth stared down at the small upturned face in astonishment.

Arabella's mouth was opening and closing. No words would come out.

'Teeny, some people don't mind jokes and some people hate them,' explained Joan, gently. 'You must please apologise to Arabella at once.'

The child went over and said sorry.

'I suppose you're only a kid,' muttered Arabella. 'But please don't do anything like that again. You will now be so kind as to spread my sleeping bag out in the sun and sit with it until it dries off. When it's completely dry, you will then roll it up and put it back in the tent.'

Arabella turned to Elizabeth.

'Sorry,' she said.

'I should think *so*!' replied Elizabeth.

Flouncing off, Arabella then called back over her shoulder to Joan:

'You could at least have stopped us two shouting at each other. No wonder Philippa didn't know who the tent monitor was supposed to be!'

It was so cruel that it brought tears to Joan's eyes.

As the two friends walked slowly away from the tent together, arm in arm, Elizabeth tried to comfort her.

'Arabella often says unkind things, Joan. You mustn't take any notice of her.'

Elizabeth was thinking hard. Her head

was still spinning from the dramatic events of the past few minutes. She was astonished that Teeny had dared to play such a trick on Arabella. Teeny was such a shy, nervous little thing! It didn't make sense, somehow.

But Joan had other things on her mind. 'I can't *help* but take notice of what Arabella said. The truth is, I'm really worried, Elizabeth,' she confessed. 'Teeny looks up to me so and I know she will want to lean on me. I'm quite frightened . . . that I'm not going to make a success of things.'

Joan looked so agitated that Elizabeth's heart went out to her.

She suddenly felt full of remorse that she had teased Joan earlier. She had not taken her friend's worries seriously. She was also very cross with herself for losing her temper with Arabella, however much she had been provoked. Arabella wasn't worth it! Nothing was worth seeing Joan unhappy.

She made a solemn vow.

'Joan, from now on I'm going to be as sweet and good-tempered with Arabella as anything. And I'll help you to make sure that Teeny doesn't do anything silly again, either. You just wait and see. Everyone in the whole camp will soon realise that you're the finest tent monitor there's ever been! I'm going to back you up all the way.'

3   Joan makes a silly mistake

As Elizabeth made her solemn vow, Joan's face lit up with pleasure. Whatever her worries, it was a great comfort to have such a loyal friend.

'Thank you, Elizabeth,' she said, softly. 'And I must try to live up to your hopes of me. I shall try not to let down any of the people in my tent.'

'You will be a fine tent monitor, just you see,' repeated Elizabeth, pleased to see that Joan looked calm and happy again. 'We'll both have to keep an eye on Teeny though, won't we? Do you think she had just *finished* filling Arabella's sleeping-bag when we surprised her in the tent? She was right next to it wasn't she? And her hands shook with fright when we appeared!'

'Why, yes, so they did,' remembered Joan. 'That must have been the reason! I had been warned to expect her to be nervy but—'

'Nobody could be as nervy as that!' agreed Elizabeth.

The two girls were walking along the top of the bank, deep in conversation.

On the opposite bank, where the boys' tents were pitched, some juniors were running along together, laughing and shouting boisterously. The girls gave them hardly a glance.

'Don't you think the whole thing was odd?' continued Elizabeth. 'It was such a strange thing for Teeny to do. She is such an unconfident little thing. Fancy her daring to try to play that trick on Arabella, of all people! You only have to look at Arabella to know that she's not the sort of person to play jokes on.'

'A girl in a higher form, as well!' agreed Joan. 'Yes, it's puzzling. But I wonder if I can guess the reason? Miss Ranger has explained to me that Teeny is desperate to make some friends. Do you think she could have read story books about camping and the jolly jokes friends play on each other? Perhaps she thought we'd all like her and think she was fun and be pleased to have her in the tent?'

'Oh, Joan, that's a clever theory!' exclaimed Elizabeth. Then she began to laugh. 'You mean, perhaps she was trying to *make friends* with Arabella—?'

'Well, at least to break the ice.'

Even Joan began to laugh now, as she saw the funny side.

'The trouble is,' sighed Elizabeth, when they had stopped laughing, 'I can see a flaw in that theory. If Teeny thought it was such a fun thing to do, why was she looking so scared—'

She got no further.

'*Look out, Joan!*' she cried.

Two figures were hurtling through the air towards them. They had launched themselves from the opposite bank and were heading straight for them!

The girls leaped back only just in time, as the flying figures thudded on to the grass in front of them, sprawled out like starfish.

'Are you all right?' gasped Joan, anxiously.

'Of course they're all right!' said Elizabeth, as a boy and girl from the junior class scrambled to their feet. 'Look where you're going, you two! You nearly landed on top of us.'

Duncan and Kitty smiled cheekily. They were two very tough little juniors, both athletic. Elizabeth glanced at the huge leap they had made and was secretly rather impressed. The two opposing banks of the old stream were high at this point, the drop between them a steep one. Why, she would rather like to try that herself!

'You're lucky you haven't hurt yourselves!' Joan was saying. 'You could have missed your footing.'

'It's easy as pie,' boasted Duncan.

'Well, you're not to do it again,' Joan told them.

'There's a footbridge down by Camp Centre,' Elizabeth pointed out, anxious to give Joan full backing. 'What's wrong with using that?'

'It's the wrong way,' grumbled Kitty, rather sulkily. 'We're going to visit one of the tents up this end.'

'Yes, that's right, we are,' agreed Duncan, looking equally put out. 'We're going to see somebody in our class, aren't we, Kitty?'

'In that case, you should have scrambled down the bank and up the other side,' Joan told them. 'And that's what you must do in future, when you don't want to use the footbridge. Is that understood?'

'Yes, Joan!'

'And turn your collars down neatly!' added Elizabeth, for good measure. 'They look messy turned up like that!'

The two friends scampered off. Joan and Elizabeth watched them for a while.

'Thanks for backing me up,' said Joan, gratefully.

'I think you managed them really well!' replied Elizabeth, turning on her heel then, impatient to be on their way. 'I wonder if we've got time to have a toasted muffin before we go to the village? I can smell them from here!'

'I'm sure we have—' Joan began.

She stopped.

'Look, Elizabeth!' she said, eagerly.

'What?' asked Elizabeth, turning back. 'Something interesting?'

'In a way, yes. Look – can you see our tent?'

Joan was pointing back the way they had come. Through a gap in the tents they could just see their own, nestling under the high brick wall. Teeny was sitting cross-legged outside the tent. She was obediently watching over Arabella's spread-out sleeping bag, waiting for it to dry. And Duncan and Kitty were running up to speak to her!

'Teeny! That's who they were on their way to see!' exclaimed Elizabeth.

'Yes, isn't it good!' said Joan, in relief. 'Teeny must be making some friends, after all.'

'Perhaps we'll be able to stop worrying about her soon,' smiled Elizabeth. 'Let's go and get our muffins now!'

As Elizabeth stood by the camp fire, swallowing delicious mouthfuls of warm muffin, she remembered some words from a famous poem that her father had once read to her. Something about – 'Bliss . . .

was it . . . in that dawn to be alive . . .'

This, she decided, was indeed bliss. How she loved it here at Whyteleafe School! How silly she'd been when she had first arrived last summer, trying to get herself sent home by being the Naughtiest Girl in the School . . . It was such a nuisance that she still had to live down that nickname. She was sorry that Philippa had overheard the quarrel with Arabella. That must have earned her a black mark! But everything was going to be all right now, surely?

Camp Centre was abuzz with activity. Some of the boys had been collecting firewood for the barbecue. Mr Leslie had finished building a fine table in the camp's Kitchen Area. Cook had arrived in her old jeep and boxes of bread rolls were being stacked on the table. Although some of their meals would be eaten in the school building, there was to be a First Night Barbecue outside this evening.

There would be sausages and grilled bacon, eaten in the open-air between crusty buttered rolls, and washed down with plenty of orange juice, apple juice or lemonade.

Elizabeth was looking forward to it with great excitement. She turned to the boy standing next to her.

'Poor old Julian, having to go home for half term!' she told Martin. Julian Holland was her great friend in the first form. 'He has no idea what he's missing!'

'There's plenty of work to do,' replied Martin, who was also in the first form. He could be rather earnest at times. He pointed to the big table. 'You and Joan are doing Kitchen Duty with me and Arabella. We've got all those bread rolls to butter!'

'Have we really?' asked Elizabeth, with interest. She had wondered what job they would be given.

Joan had been talking to Susan, the other second form monitor. They had been in a huddle together over their timetables. All the tent monitors had been given one of the typewritten lists in advance. It was their responsibility to see that the members of their tent were at all times punctual for Camp Duties.

'Elizabeth! Here a minute!' Joan called, as Susan walked away.

As soon as Elizabeth rejoined her friend, she could see that something was wrong.

'I've made a silly mistake,' she said, looking agitated. She handed Elizabeth the timetable and pointed to the first day rota. 'I looked so quickly, I thought that was a 6. But it isn't! It's a 5—'

'So it is,' replied Elizabeth, peering at it. 'It's a bit smudgy. You could easily mistake it for a 6—'

'So we've got to report for Kitchen Duty not at six o'clock but at five!' Joan was saying. 'And that's less than half an hour away!'

'Well, don't look so worried, Joan. We all make mistakes!' said Elizabeth cheerfully. Secretly she felt rather pleased. A trip to the village today had never been high on her list, not when they were still enjoying settling into camp! 'We'll just have to go and get your new torch batteries tomorrow, after all,' she smiled. 'It was lucky you noticed in time—'

Because I don't want any more black marks against my name! Elizabeth was thinking privately.

'Oh, don't be feeble, Elizabeth!' interrupted Joan, sharply. 'Of course we must get the batteries today. We can't possibly leave it till tomorrow!'

'But—'

'No "buts"! Come on, quickly, we've got to hurry!'

Joan grabbed hold of her friend's hand

and hauled her towards the footbridge which joined up the two halves of the camp.

'If we go up past the boys' tents, there's a short cut through to the back drive! Then it's only a few minutes down to the village. I've got my purse with me!'

'Joan, I don't think we've got enough time!' protested Elizabeth, puffing to keep up with her friend. 'Even if the batteries do run out tonight, it won't really matter, will it?'

'Of course it will!' exclaimed Joan. She seemed in a slight panic. 'Supposing Teeny wakes up in the night and wants something . . . If you're tent monitor, you *must* have a working torch. I'm sure it's one of the rules. *Please*, Elizabeth!' Joan shot her friend an imploring glance. 'We can run all the way there and all the way back. You know what a fast runner you are! You promised you'd help me to be a good monitor—'

'Of course,' nodded Elizabeth. She could see now that this was really important to Joan. 'Let's run really fast then. Let's break the world speed record!'

They pelted over the wooden footbridge and up the field, past the boys' tents, the summer breeze blowing through their hair. It was really exhilarating, running as fast as this! thought Elizabeth.

But it took them some time to find the short cut through some bushes that led into the school's back drive. The leaves had grown and all the bushes looked the same. By the time they reached the school gates, Elizabeth knew they were not going to make it to the village and back by five o'clock.

4 Elizabeth remembers her vow

As they came through the school gates and pounded along by the road, on the grass verge, Elizabeth glanced at her watch with a sinking heart. This was such a mad idea of Joan's. They had not even reached the first corner yet!

But Joan was striding out, keeping just ahead of Elizabeth, her teeth gritted.

Then, rounding the first corner, Elizabeth let out a whoop of joy.

Of course! The garage shop!

'Look, Joan, the garage is open!' she cried out, in relief. 'We won't have to go all the way to the village, after all!'

'I always get my batteries at the

hardware store—' began Joan.

'I tell you, the shop at the garage sells them!' protested Elizabeth. 'How silly of me to forget. I went there once with Julian! He needed some for a model he was making.'

Recovering their breath, the girls picked their way through the forecourt of the petrol station. It was very busy indeed today, packed with cars waiting for petrol.

The hopeful look on Joan's face quickly faded when she saw the long queue of people in the garage shop.

'Oh, Elizabeth, it will take all day! Are you sure they sell them? Don't you think it would be better if we just raced straight on to the village—?'

'No, I don't!' said Elizabeth firmly. It was such a warm afternoon. The run had already made her hot and sticky. 'It will be much nicer standing in a queue than running along by the dusty old road. Have you got any spare money, Joan? Perhaps we can get an ice cream as well.'

'I really think we *should* run on—'

But Elizabeth looked resolute and went and stood at the back of the queue. On this matter, at least, she felt that Joan was being unreasonable. Joan had no choice but to come and stand beside her. She could see that Elizabeth had no intention of budging. And, of course, it was strictly forbidden for children to go to the village on their own.

The queue moved at a snail's pace. Joan fretted and frowned the whole while. At one point, the shop manager disappeared for minutes on end to help a driver who was having trouble with the air machine.

'Sorry about that, folks,' he apologised, when he returned. 'The poor man had a flat tyre!'

When Joan and Elizabeth finally got to

the front of the queue, a horrible shock awaited.

'I'm sorry, girls,' said the man, coming back with some batteries. 'These are the only ones we stock here. If you need the bigger ones you'll have to go down to the village.'

Elizabeth could have died of shame!

Joan was wonderfully sporting about it.

'Don't be upset!' she said, sweetly. 'It's no use crying over spilt milk. We'll just have to run all the harder now, won't we?'

Joan had no intention of being defeated. She was still determined to buy her new batteries!

They ran all the way to the hardware shop in the village, where there was no queue at all and the correct batteries were in stock. Then they raced all the way back to school.

They were terribly late.

It was long past five o'clock.

Martin and Arabella had buttered a whole mountain of rolls without them. They were standing by the big table in the Kitchen Area, with the buttered rolls piled high in front of them.

'We were waiting and waiting for you to come!' complained Martin.

'We've just this minute finished. We had to do them all on our own, every single one!' said Arabella. 'It's not fair. You were supposed to be here at five o'clock!' she added, very loudly.

Miss Ranger appeared.

'So there you are, Joan. Where *have* you been this past half hour?'

She looked very angry.

'I needed some new batteries for my torch, Miss Ranger,' began Joan. 'I'm so sorry, I—'

'That's no excuse, Joan. You know how important it is we keep to the timetable at all times, if camp is to run smoothly. And you a tent monitor! You're supposed to set a good example—'

Arabella was listening in the background, looking smug.

But it was not Arabella's face that Elizabeth was glancing at. It was Joan's. To see the distress on her best friend's face was almost unbearable!

Elizabeth remembered her solemn vow. She pushed herself forward.

'Please, Miss Ranger, it wasn't Joan's fault,' she burst forth. 'It was entirely *my* fault! I made Joan stop at the garage shop and there was a long queue and they didn't have the right batteries! I should have listened to Joan. We should have headed straight for the right shop, in the village, the way she wanted us to, instead of me being so lazy, and then we would have been back here much quicker!'

'I see,' replied the teacher, gazing at Elizabeth and recalling her Naughtiest

Girl nickname. For a moment, Elizabeth wondered if she were going to be punished. But then—

'Thank you very much for owning up, Elizabeth,' said Miss Ranger, with a nod. 'That was quite the right thing to do.'

Elizabeth felt a warm glow.

It was worth getting into trouble herself, to have helped Joan. Now nobody would think Joan was a bad tent monitor and Arabella could wipe the smug smile off her face.

But, to Elizabeth's dismay, Miss Ranger turned back to Joan immediately.

And she proceeded to give her a stern lecture.

'You should know by now, Joan, that Elizabeth can be headstrong. And she is younger than you, too. Just because she is your friend, that is no reason to forget that you are also her tent monitor. At camp, where everybody has more freedom, that carries very special responsibilities. You must remember those responsibilities in future and assert your authority at all times.'

For Joan, it was mortifying.

For Elizabeth, it was completely infuriating.

She had got herself into trouble, and earned a black mark, all for nothing! It had not helped to get Joan out of trouble, after all. If anything, it had got her in deeper! It was *not* the outcome that Elizabeth had intended.

The pleased expression on Arabella's face didn't help her temper, either. She would no doubt be spreading the story round the camp with glee.

Was Teeny really going to wake in the night, wondered Elizabeth, as Joan feared? Was Joan *really* going to need those silly new torch batteries? After all, it looked as though Teeny had already made friends with Duncan and Kitty at camp. Now that the junior girl had made some friends of her own, reasoned Elizabeth, she would soon stop being so dependent on Joan. She would stop going around looking so nervous and fearful and Joan would be able to relax!

But Joan did not relax.

She didn't seem to enjoy the barbecue at all. It was not just the telling-off from Miss Ranger. There was more to it than that. Elizabeth felt sure she knew what the reason must be.

Duncan and Kitty had not made friends with Teeny, after all.

5 Quite a different Teeny

The other juniors all ignored Teeny. Duncan and Kitty rushed happily around at the barbecue with their friends. None of them took the slightest notice of the little girl.

At one point, Duncan bounded up to Elizabeth, munching a bacon roll, looking cheeky.

'Mr Leslie says we can if we want to, Elizabeth!' he said, through a mouthful of bread.

'Don't speak with your mouth full, Duncan!' said Elizabeth. 'Can do *what* if you want to?'

'While we're at camp!'

'Do what while you're at camp?' repeated Elizabeth.

'Wear our collars up, of course!' he said, and went bounding off again.

As Duncan rejoined his friends, Elizabeth saw that at least five of them were following the same fashion. Their blue school sports shirts were buttoned to the neck and the collars turned up. The rest of the school wore the shirts open-necked, the collars neat and flat. How silly, thought Elizabeth. She smiled to herself. It must be the latest craze in the junior class. But she had neither noticed nor cared this time. Her eyes were elsewhere, watching Teeny closely. They returned to Teeny now.

What was wrong with the child? She was so nervous and jumpy. She seemed frightened of her own shadow! She stuck close to Joan's side all the time, following her around like a puppy-dog! Poor Joan looked more strained by the minute, weighed down by the responsibility.

Elizabeth felt guilty that she had

questioned Joan's decision to get the batteries. Perhaps it really was important, after all. It was Teeny's first night at camp tonight. If she had a bad, sleepless night then Joan would need the torch, to be able to attend to her.

'And if that happens, I shall speak to Miss Ranger about it in the morning!' decided Elizabeth. 'Joan's much too brave to go bleating to Miss Ranger on her own behalf but I shall say something. And then Miss Ranger will realise how important it was for us to run down to the village and how responsible Joan was being!'

That thought cheered Elizabeth up considerably.

A little fantasy ran through her mind in which Teeny was tossing and turning in her sleeping bag that night, until Joan came and sat beside her and held her hand, quietly reading her a story by the light of the torch. The child then dropping off into a deep, contented sleep . . .

Then, in the morning, fantasised Elizabeth, she would find Miss Ranger and quietly explain how wonderful Joan had been and how important it had been that her torch was working. And Miss Ranger would run anxiously to find Joan, to apologise. *Please forgive me, Joan. What you and Elizabeth did was much more important than buttering bread rolls. I can see you are a very fine tent monitor indeed . . .*

'Elizabeth! There are some sausages left!' cried Kathleen, breaking into the reverie. The rosy-cheeked first former ran over and grabbed Elizabeth's hand. 'Come on, hurry, they'll soon be all gone!'

Elizabeth enjoyed herself after that.

Food tasted so delicious eaten out of doors, around the camp fire. The sweet smell of woodsmoke made her feel thirsty but there were plenty of cold drinks to be had. Elizabeth liked the apple juice best. They were all being spoiled tonight, as a special treat. There was some excitement when little Kitty was stung by a huge bumblebee. But she was very brave and didn't cry at all. Rita took her to the first aid tent, where Matron treated the sting and soon made it better.

After that Mr Lewis, the school music master, came down to Camp Centre with an accordion which he squeezed and played jolly tunes on. Then they had a sing-song round the dying embers of the fire. It was all very exciting.

At the end of the evening, Elizabeth and Joan each took one of Teeny's hands and led her back to the tent. They were careful to step over the guy ropes of Miss Ranger's tent, on the way. The teacher had her own private tent, a smart little green one.

'It's nice to think we have Miss Ranger so close at hand, isn't it, Teeny?' said Joan.

'I'm not scared,' said Teeny. 'Not when you're going to be in the tent with me, Joan.'

Soon Joan was settling the girl down into her sleeping bag. The juniors had been allowed to stay up late tonight. Teeny Wilson had had a long day.

'It's going to be a busy day tomorrow, Teeny,' said Joan, looking at her timetable. 'After breakfast, we are going to have a Meeting.'

'A proper Meeting, with William and Rita in charge?' asked Teeny, wide-eyed. 'Just like we have in school?'

'That's right,' nodded Joan. 'Except we will sit on ground sheets, in rows, and there won't be a platform. And also Miss Ranger hopes the Meeting will be nice and short. There hasn't been much time for any Complaints or Grumbles yet, has there?'

'No.' Guiltily the child stole a glance at Arabella's sleeping bag. It was neatly rolled up in the tent now. Arabella had not got back yet. 'No, I suppose not.'

'And tomorrow afternoon, Teeny, we're going on a nature walk over in the woods. I will be in charge of you. We'll take paper bags with us and see how many interesting things we can collect. Won't that be fun?'

Teeny peered over the top of her sleeping bag. Elizabeth thought she saw sudden fear in the child's eyes.

'I don't think I want to go to the woods, Joan. Do we have to go? Couldn't we stay in the tent, instead? I've got my playing cards with me. We could play a game of Snap.'

'No, Teeny.' Joan suddenly sounded very weary. 'We have to keep to the timetable. It's much more fun in the fresh air, anyway! We can play Snap some other time, if it rains.'

Elizabeth felt sorry for her friend. Poor Joan! She had been stuck with Teeny all evening. She took her responsibilities so much to heart.

'Why don't you go off and have a chat with Susan now, Joan?' she suggested nobly. 'I'll stay here and keep Teeny company. Go on!'

'Perhaps I will!' she said, gratefully. 'It would be rather nice to see Susan. She's promised to lend me a book.'

As Joan ducked away out of the tent, Elizabeth picked up her rolled-up sleeping bag, placed it by Teeny and sat on it.

She was remembering the little daydream she had had earlier.

'Have you got a favourite book with you, Teeny?' she asked. 'Would you like me to read you a bedtime story?'

It might help Teeny to get to sleep, being read a story, Elizabeth had decided. Though not by torchlight, of course, for it was still light outside and the tent flap was rolled back.

'Ooh, thanks, Elizabeth!'

In the next five minutes, Elizabeth very quickly discovered that her earlier daydream was certainly not going to come true.

In fact, it could not have been more wide of the mark!

After finding a book and handing it to Elizabeth, the junior girl squirmed down happily into her sleeping bag. She smiled and gave a contented sigh. This was quite a different Teeny. For the first time, all the strain seemed to have left her little face.

'Oh, I do love it in here!' she told Elizabeth. 'It's so warm and cosy and soon it will be dark. It's going to be lovely snuggled up in my sleeping bag in the dark. I wish I could stay snuggled up in our cosy house like this all the time!'

Elizabeth started to read out loud.

She was only two pages into the story when she heard a very gentle snoring sound. Teeny's eyes were closed. She was already in a deep, sound sleep.

'What a fuss about nothing,' thought Elizabeth. 'Teeny likes it in the tent!'

And Teeny remained sound asleep for the rest of the night.

The only person to enjoy the use of the torch was Joan! She had awoken suddenly, just after it had got dark and had used her torch to read in bed.

Elizabeth woke in the night to hear Arabella complaining bitterly.

'How are the rest of us supposed to get any sleep with that wretched torch on!' she whispered loudly. 'I don't care if Joan *is* the tent monitor, it's not fair of her to keep other people awake.'

Bleary-eyed, Elizabeth sat up to see what the fuss was about.

Joan was fast asleep. Her book and torch had fallen from her grasp. The torch had rolled along and was lying next to the book. The torch had been left on, its powerful beam lighting up the tent!

Joan had been reading in bed and had carelessly fallen asleep without switching it off!

'It's all right, Arabella, I'll fix it!' whispered Elizabeth, squirming out of her sleeping bag into the cool night air. She tiptoed across to Joan's side, clicked off the torch, then stumbled her way back through the darkness to her sleeping bag.

As Elizabeth wriggled back into her sleeping bag and fumbled with the zip, she couldn't help feeling cross. Now she was cold!

It suddenly seemed even more ridiculous, all the fuss Joan had made about getting the new torch batteries. Why, they weren't needed at all! Teeny loved it in the tent. She was in a deep, deep sleep. Even Arabella's complaining hadn't woken her.

Meanwhile, Joan had not even been trying to conserve the new batteries. Far from it. She had been really careless.

It was really very lucky that the beam of light had woken up Arabella. Otherwise Joan's precious new batteries, which had caused them so much trouble, would have been completely dead by the morning!

Sometime later that night, Elizabeth was again woken by Arabella. She was still complaining – and this time more loudly.

'I'm freezing!' came the petulant voice. 'I'm absolutely freezing. Joan, can you hear me? I'm freezing, I tell you.'

Elizabeth blinked and sat up. Joan was awake herself this time. She, too, was sitting up. Only Teeny, at the back of the tent next to Elizabeth, snored on happily.

For a moment, Elizabeth was puzzled. It was the middle of the night, the coldest and darkest time, and yet she could see!

Instead of it being pitch dark inside the tent, as it had been earlier, everything was bathed in a pale light. She could see Arabella and Joan clearly, sitting up in their sleeping bags on the other side of the tent.

'You've opened the tent flap!' Arabella accused Joan.

Even as Arabella said it, Elizabeth suddenly realised that the tent flap was rolled back and tied in its daytime position. She could see the moon and the stars outside, hanging in a bright, clear night sky! They were shining into the tent! It was a beautiful sky, thought Elizabeth.

'Teeny needs some fresh air, Arabella,' hissed Joan. 'Please keep your voice down. You'll wake the other two.'

'Fresh air? It's cold! It's coming right on my face.'

'Lie down and go to sleep at once, Arabella,' replied Joan. 'It's rather stuffy in the tent with four people sleeping in it.

As tent monitor, I have decided to open the flap. I am in charge and I must ask you to lie down and go back to sleep.'

'How can I go to sleep—?' began Arabella, her voice getting squeaky. 'I'm right next to it!'

Elizabeth listened, in consternation. It didn't seem to her to be stuffy in the tent, not in the least. But Joan was right, she *was* their tent monitor. Miss Ranger had told her to exert her authority. And now that was exactly what she was doing . . .

On the other hand, whatever the rights and wrongs of it, there was going to be an awful rumpus in a minute if Joan wasn't careful.

'It's all right, Arabella!' hissed Elizabeth. 'We can change places. I don't mind some fresh air. May we change places, Joan?'

'Of course, Elizabeth,' replied her friend, in gratitude. 'Arabella, please go and sleep in Elizabeth's place, now that you've woken her up. And do *not* wake Teeny up. You've made quite enough noise already.'

Grumbling quietly, Arabella did as she was told.

In her new place, next to the open tent flap, Elizabeth tried to settle down and get warm and go back to sleep.

It took her quite some time.

'*I do think Arabella's got a point*, she thought, shivering slightly. *It's much too cold here, with the tent flap open. Oh dear. I do hope Joan's not going to find the tent stuffy every night. I didn't think it was stuffy at all!*

Elizabeth slept fitfully and was the last person in the tent to awake next morning. Gentle sunshine was now filtering in through the open tent flap. Joan and Teeny had gone to wash and clean their teeth. Arabella was about to follow suit.

'Fancy offering to sleep there, Elizabeth!' she commented. 'You should have backed me up. We should have insisted that Joan close the flap. I was still cold, even on the other side of the tent. I'm not going to put up with this every night.'

'You may have to. Joan's our tent monitor, not you, Arabella!' said Elizabeth, loyally.

Arabella's mouth set in a thin, stubborn line.

'Have you forgotten there's a Meeting this morning, Elizabeth? I have every intention of making a Complaint!'

6 *Elizabeth begins to lose patience*

At Whyteleafe School, the children made many decisions for themselves. A weekly Meeting was held, attended by the whole school. The Meeting was run not by the teachers, but by William and Rita, the head-boy and girl, assisted by twelve school monitors who sat just behind them.

It was a kind of parliament. Problems were discussed, rules and regulations made. At the same time, it was a little 'court', too, with William and Rita as the judges and the monitors, the jury. Wrong-doing had to be reported. If it were serious, it was written in the Book. The Meeting would then decide what action should be taken. Of course, the joint headmistresses and the senior master always sat at the back of the hall, as observers. But they rarely took any part in the Meetings. The children were expected to face up to their own faults bravely and work out the best way of dealing with them.

Elizabeth had hated the Meetings when she first came to Whyteleafe School. They had made it so difficult for her to be naughty! These days, however, she rather enjoyed them.

But she feared that this morning's Meeting might be less enjoyable than usual.

It would be held at Camp Centre, as soon as the boys and girls had washed up their breakfast things. There had been cornflakes and milk this morning, followed by plenty more buttered rolls, washed down with a mug of hot tea. Each pupil was responsible for their own enamel mug, bowl and plate, as well as their cutlery.

They queued at the two stand-pipes set up in the Kitchen Area and swilled their mugs and bowls clean in jets of cold water. Mr Leslie had linked the camp site into the mains water supply, which already ran to the nearby stables.

He had also constructed a simple drainage system which took the waste water down to the empty stream bed. Elizabeth thought it was very clever.

It really was like a secret village here!

On this pleasant, sweet-scented morning, Elizabeth could not bring herself to tell Joan what Arabella had said. She was hoping that Arabella would change her mind. Joan had enough to worry about, for already Teeny was hanging around her again. Gone was the happy, relaxed little thing who had been in the tent last night. She was back to her usual jumpy self, with that funny half-scared look behind the big glasses.

It occurred to Elizabeth that Teeny would not be looking forward to the Meeting, either. She must be wondering if Arabella were going to make a Complaint about the sleeping-bag joke, or at the very least, a Grumble. As Elizabeth dried up her cereal bowl, flicking a fly away with the tea-towel, she puzzled again about that strange incident.

Whatever possessed Teeny to try to play such a trick? she thought. *I still don't understand it.*

Would Arabella make Complaints about both Joan *and* Teeny at the Meeting? Elizabeth was very much hoping that she would think better of it. There she was now, sitting on a log in the sunshine, talking cheerfully to Belinda. She seemed in a good mood. The night was over. It was the nice, warm daytime again!

I think I'll go and speak to her, and be friendly, Elizabeth decided, remembering her promise to Joan. *I'll suggest we ask Joan if the four of us can take a vote about having the tent flap open at nights. That would be a much better way of settling it.*

But before she could get Arabella alone, the whistle blew. It was time for the Meeting.

All the children went and sat in rows, on the ground sheets. Facing them, William and Rita sat on upturned logs behind a camping table. The big Book was on the table in front of them. Seated cross-legged alongside them, also facing the audience, were the sixteen tent monitors, Joan amongst them. On canvas chairs, somewhere at the back, sat three grown-ups. Instead of Miss Belle and Miss Best and Mr Johns, as it would have been indoors, it was Miss Ranger, Mr Leslie and Matron. Apart from that, and the fact that they were out of doors (and a great number of children had gone home for half term) it was just like a proper Meeting! And William even had to bang on the table for silence, as usual. He did this with a wooden mallet used for driving in tent pegs. He had forgotten to bring the gavel.

The Meeting was much shorter than usual.

There was no money to be shared out. That had been done just before half term. There was only one Grumble.

'Please, the zip of my sleeping bag keeps sticking,' said John McTavish. 'It's such a nuisance.'

'Sort it out with your tent monitor. There's probably a piece of lining caught in it!' replied William, at once. 'That's not a proper Grumble, John. What can the Meeting possibly do about it?'

Everybody laughed and John hastily sat down.

But Arabella duly made her Complaint, as promised.

Just as Rita was about to close the Meeting, she rose hesitantly to her feet. Elizabeth noticed Teeny blanch. But Arabella had no intention of complaining about the sleeping-bag joke. She had better fish to fry.

'I'm sorry to have to bring this up, William and Rita,' she said, looking her demurest and most doll-like. 'It's really a little embarrassing because it's a Complaint about something our tent monitor did last night.'

Elizabeth saw Joan stiffen.

'Very well, Arabella,' said the head-girl. 'Let us hear your Complaint.'

With considerable dramatic skill, Arabella told the Meeting about the freezing cold draught that had woken her in the night, her shock at finding the tent flap had been tied back and her monitor's insistence that it should remain open for the rest of the night.

William and Rita exchanged uneasy glances. They were well used to Arabella's Complaints. Often they were trivial and almost always shrill. But this morning her tone was calm and measured.

'That is a perfectly reasonable Complaint, even though it is about a tent monitor,' agreed William. 'Let us first of all hear what Joan has to say. Sit down, please, Arabella.'

Joan seemed to be frozen. There was a helpless expression on her face. Susan had to give her a nudge, to make her stand up.

'I – I just thought the tent seemed rather stuffy, that's all,' she said feebly. 'I thought perhaps it would be better for the four of us to have some fresh air.'

Elizabeth sat there, curling up with embarrassment on Joan's behalf. Some of the campers were whispering and giving Joan surprised looks. Instead of trying to put up a spirited defence, Joan had made her excuse very lamely. It was almost as though she, herself, thought that what she was saying sounded rather silly!

And for the first time, Elizabeth realised it only too plainly. It *was* silly. It was ridiculous. It had been freezing in that draught last night!

As Joan sat down again, William and Rita asked the rest of the tent monitors to come into a huddle while they debated the issue.

Joan sat apart, looking abject, while the discussion took place. All around Elizabeth there was giggling and chattering, and people saying *Brrrrr*! It always added spice to Meetings when somebody made a proper Complaint.

Soon, the tent monitors returned to their places. William banged the mallet on the table.

'Silence, please. We are all agreed that the bell tents are designed to be closed at night. This stops insects flying in. There are adequate fresh-air vents in the canvas. After all, they were made for the British Army's desert campaign! Stand up again, please, Joan.'

Joan did so.

'Arabella's Complaint is Upheld. If you find the tent a little stuffy, perhaps your sleeping bag is too heavy, Joan,' he added, sympathetically. 'I'm sure Matron might be able to find you a lighter one, if you ask her.'

The Meeting broke up.

Elizabeth hurried over to join Joan and linked arms with her. She hated to see her so upset.

'I should have warned you! Arabella told me she was going to make a Complaint but I was hoping she would think better of it.'

'It wouldn't have made any difference, if you had,' said Joan, in a dull voice. 'It was fair enough. Perfectly fair.'

'Oh, then you don't mind if we have the flap closed tonight?' asked Elizabeth, unable to hide her relief.

'It will have to be, won't it?' sighed Joan. 'I can't have some of you feeling cold . . .'

'But Teeny was perfectly all right, Joan!' exclaimed Elizabeth, to cheer her friend up. 'I know you were worried about the tent being stuffy for Teeny's sake. But she slept like a baby, didn't she? She was fine. You didn't even need the torch for her! That's good, isn't it—?'

Elizabeth broke off. Miss Ranger was walking up to them.

The teacher spoke quietly to Joan.

'Let me explain something,' she said. 'I know I told you yesterday that you must always be sure to assert your authority, to show exactly who is tent monitor. But by that I meant you must be sure to keep Elizabeth in order! If you try to assert your authority in an unreasonable way, as you appear to have done with Arabella, then you will lose your tent-mates' respect.'

'Yes, Miss Ranger,' replied Joan.

As the two friends walked back to the tent together, Elizabeth felt helpless. She was so determined that everyone should see what a fine tent monitor Joan was. She had even earned a black mark with Miss Ranger, covering up for her. But she could see Joan's confidence ebbing away in front of her eyes. Had Elizabeth's best efforts all been in vain? Things had certainly got off to a very bad start.

As if to prove Miss Ranger's point, Arabella's respect for Joan was now very low. After the triumph of having her Complaint upheld at today's Meeting, there was no stopping her!

When the friends arrived back at the tent, they found her already arranging some of her things round the sides, humming cheerfully. Teeny was with her.

'Thank you for not telling on me at the Meeting,' the junior was saying, gratefully.

'Oh, that's all right, Teeny,' replied Arabella, nonchalantly. 'I think we should have my mirror here, don't you? We can prop it up in the middle, against the tent pole.'

The vain first former had been feeling lost without her favourite mirror. Usually it hung by her bed in the dormitory. If she stood far enough back she could almost get a full-length view in it. She had carefully wrapped it and staggered down to the camp site with it. She had been puzzling ever since whether she would need Joan's permission to put it up in the tent.

'Hey, you can't put a mirror up in here!' protested Elizabeth. 'It'll get in the way. We'll all trip over it.'

'But we *need* a mirror in here, don't we,

Joan?' said Arabella, turning to the tent monitor.

Joan hesitated. Without even waiting for her reply, Arabella knelt down by the central tent pole and carefully propped the mirror there. She preened herself in it.

'There!' she said. 'We all want to make sure we look nice, don't we, Teeny? Just because we're at camp, that's no excuse for looking scruffy. I've brought plenty of different clothes—'

'We can see that—' began Elizabeth, hotly. They were stacked all round the sides of the tent. Then she stopped.

She mustn't lose her temper with Arabella. She had promised Joan that. It would only make Joan's life more difficult.

'Please let's have a mirror up in the tent, Joan!' begged Teeny, coming and holding her hand. 'It'll make it more like our little house than ever!'

'You can have it up if you want,

Arabella,' decided Joan.

'Oh, thank you, Joan. I was sure you'd agree!' replied Arabella, smiling sweetly.

Elizabeth glowered and left the tent.

Later, Joan apologised to Elizabeth.

'I only agreed to please Teeny,' she said. 'Have you noticed how happy she is in the tent? She's like a different person. It's as though she feels safe when she's in our little house, as she calls it.'

So Joan had realised it, too.

'I wonder why she doesn't mix with the other juniors?' continued Joan. 'Do you think she could be being bullied?'

'I'm sure not,' shrugged Elizabeth. 'She's been at Whyteleafe since the beginning of term. There would have been some sign of it by now. Somebody would have seen something.'

'But there is *something* not right,' sighed Joan.

In her present mood, Elizabeth was not

sure if she cared. Far from it being fun to have a little junior to look after in the tent, it had become a problem. Joan, so kind and conscientious, had become a hopeless worrier since being put in charge of Teeny! That was at the root of things. Everything that had gone wrong had been due, in one way or another, to Teeny, decided Elizabeth.

Drat the little creature, she thought, crossly. *I'm beginning to wish Joan had never set eyes on her.*

That afternoon, there was worse to come.

7 Teeny has an unhelpful fall

Elizabeth had not slept well that first night but Joan had fared even worse. By the end of the morning, she began to look rather tired. Just how tired Joan was, Elizabeth was soon to discover.

Elizabeth was sitting in the school dining hall, with Teeny, eating a delicious meal of hot pie, with buttered new potatoes and carrots. It tasted good. The joint heads had decided that every day at one o'clock, the children should come indoors for their main hot meal of the day.

But where was Joan? wondered Elizabeth.

At midday, Rita had announced to the campers that any girl who wished to have a hot shower before lunch could go up to school early. Joan had thought that seemed a fine idea and hurried off. Elizabeth wasn't bothered.

'I'll meet you in the dining hall, then, Joan. I'll bring Teeny with me.'

'Save me a place! I expect there will be a long queue for the showers,' was Joan's reply.

Elizabeth had saved Joan a place but her friend had still not appeared. All the other girls were back from their showers and were halfway through lunch! Whatever could have happened to Joan?

She'll miss out on the first course altogether, if she's not careful, thought Elizabeth, in alarm. *The queue for pudding's starting to form now*.

She gobbled down her last new potato and got up from the table.

'I'm just slipping off to find Joan,' she told Teeny. 'Now, you be sure and eat up all your food.'

'She must have forgotten the time,' said Teeny solemnly.

But the showers were silent and deserted. There was no sign of Joan in there. Puzzled, Elizabeth scratched her brown curly head. Where should she look now?

Perhaps Joan had gone to her dormitory, to find something she had forgotten to pack – ? Perhaps she was having a problem finding it . . .

Elizabeth bounded up the stairs to Joan's dormitory and threw open the door.

'Joan!' she exclaimed, in amazement.

Her friend lay on top of the bed, fast asleep!

'Joan, wake up! Wake up!' Elizabeth shook Joan's shoulder. 'You've fallen asleep! There's delicious hot pie for lunch and you'll miss it, at this rate!'

Joan woke up, looked startled, and sat bolt upright.

'Whatever time is it? I felt so sleepy after my shower. I only meant to have a little nap – oh, Elizabeth! I'm so sorry you've had to come looking for me! The fact is, I didn't sleep very well last night.'

'I wondered where you'd got to!' laughed Elizabeth, in relief.

Except Joan's lack of sleep was no laughing matter, as Elizabeth soon came to discover. On the nature walk in the woods that afternoon, she thought that she had never seen her friend so exhausted. She kept on yawning and there were dark rings under her eyes.

Poor Joan! she thought. *By the look of her, she hardly got a wink of sleep at all in the tent last night. Worrying about Teeny and everything, I suppose.*

Miss Ranger and Mr Leslie had escorted all the boys and girls along the country lane at the back of the school and into the woods. They all walked with the teachers for a time and had fun naming different flowers and watching birds.

Then, brown paper bags were handed out.

'You're all to scatter for half an hour,' smiled Miss Ranger. 'See how many different leaves you can find.' The pretty little woods boasted a splendid variety of trees. 'When we get back to camp, we'll see if we can identify them all. Let's see who can find the most!'

'And no need to go up trees,' said Mr Leslie. 'You will find plenty of leaves growing low down and some on the ground, as well. When I blow the whistle you are all to return here.'

The teachers then reminded all members of the junior class that they must stay close to their tent monitors and obey their orders.

Teeny was full of energy after her good night's sleep. She kept running up to Joan and showing her the leaves she was finding. Elizabeth collected some as well. To her relief, Arabella had decided to go off with Philippa and Mandy, the junior in the next door tent.

Joan, pleased to see that Teeny was enjoying herself after all, went and sat on a mossy bank. It was beneath an oak tree, in a lovely sunny spot, on the edge of a dell.

'I don't think I can go another step,' she said, leaning back against the tree trunk. 'Let's have a little rest.'

Elizabeth came and sat down beside her. Both girls tilted their faces towards the sun. It was lovely to feel its warmth on their cheeks and to hear the breeze rustling through the leaves of the oak tree. Teeny walked round the tree and found an oak leaf to add to her collection.

'Coming over here with us, Teeny?' called a voice.

Kitty and Duncan appeared on the other

side of the dell. They were waving to
Teeny to come and join them, in a friendly
fashion.

Elizabeth and Joan glanced at each
other eagerly. Yesterday they had been
disappointed when Duncan and Kitty's
visit to the tent had come to nothing. But
surely there could be no mistaking the
situation today? The two children were
trying to get to know Teeny better.

'Some friends from your class!' said
Elizabeth, pleased.

'Would you like to go and play with
them?' asked Joan, gently.

The little girl stood motionless. She
clenched and unclenched her fists two or
three times, as though trying to screw up
courage. Then, coming to a decision, she
nodded. What a funny, nervous little thing
she was, thought Elizabeth.

'Off you go, then!' smiled Joan.

Even as the little girl walked slowly

down into the bumpy dell to join her classmates, Joan gave a huge yawn and her eyes closed, thankfully.

'If you don't mind, Elizabeth, I'm going to snatch a nap. Will you keep an eye on them for me?'

'Of course!' replied Elizabeth.

Within moments, Joan had dozed off!

It was so comfortable and warm on the mossy bank, thought Elizabeth, she would have liked a snooze herself. She closed her eyes and leaned against the huge tree trunk, enjoying the feel of the rough bark in the small of her back. With eyes closed, she could hear the murmur of voices as Duncan, Kitty and Teeny talked together in the dell. What a happy sound, she thought. Was Teeny making a real effort to mix with her classmates, at last?

In her sleepy state, it was a few moments before Elizabeth realised that the murmur of voices was becoming fainter, fading

into the distance . . . She opened her eyes
instantly, in time to glimpse the three
figures disappearing amongst some trees
on the other side of the dell.

'I'd better creep after them!' she thought.
'Just to keep an eye on them. I mustn't
spoil any fun though, not when Teeny's
making friends at last.'

Leaving Joan fast asleep, Elizabeth
tiptoed across the dell and into the trees.
From the sound of the children's voices,
she could tell they had stopped somewhere.
As she drew nearer, she darted from tree to
tree, in order not to be seen. There was
no sign of Kitty's tent monitor, nor of
Duncan's.

'The little imps must have given them
the slip,' thought Elizabeth, smiling to
herself. 'But I don't suppose they can be
very far away.'

She pulled up behind some rhododen-
dron bushes and peered through the masses

of blossom. Now she had a clear view of
the children!

'I'll go first, then Kitty, then you!'
Duncan was shouting.

Elizabeth stared. The three juniors were
up a tree. They were all sitting astride
a long low bough which stretched out
horizontally, a few feet above the ground.
Duncan was moving into a crouching
position.

'Watch me do it, Teeny!' he was
shouting. 'It's easy-peasy!'

He jumped from the end of the bough
and landed in the long grass below, quite
comfortably.

'Now me!' cried Kitty excitedly,
bumping along to the end of the bough
and doing likewise.

Elizabeth was too far back to stop them.

Besides, it looked a very easy jump and
rather fun, she thought. Her main emotion
was relief, at the sight of Teeny having fun

with her classmates at last!

'Now you, Teeny!' Kitty was calling up. 'Do it just like we did. Dare you!'

The bespectacled junior was bumping out along the bough, very, very slowly. Halfway along, she looked down and seemed to freeze.

'Come on, Teeny!' encouraged Duncan.

From her hiding place, Elizabeth silently urged her on. *Yes, come on, Teeny. What have you stopped for? It's easy!* She wanted to shout it out loud. *Come on, Teeny. You know you can do it!* She could tell from the look on Duncan and Kitty's faces that they wanted Teeny to succeed, too.

'I can't!' Teeny suddenly cried out. 'I can't do it!'

Panic-stricken, she tried to turn round on the bough, to go back the way she had come. Duncan and Kitty were shouting at her . . .

'Don't do that! Don't be a baby!'

'You'll fall if you try that! Don't be such a coward, Teeny!'

Teeny just carried on trying to twist round, getting her legs in a hopeless tangle. She slithered and slipped – and overbalanced.

'Aaah!'

'*Teeny!*'

Even as Elizabeth was running towards her, Teeny came toppling down off the bough, her glasses flying through the air.

'Teeny! Are you all right?' exclaimed Elizabeth.

Duncan and Kitty looked on in dismay.

Elizabeth helped the little girl to her feet and dusted her down. She was shaken but unhurt.

Elizabeth found her glasses for her.

'Thank you, Elizabeth,' said Teeny, taking them. She looked very shamefaced. 'I was such a coward! It wasn't Duncan and Kitty's fault.'

'I know it wasn't,' said Elizabeth. 'I saw what happened—'

Duncan and Kitty exchanged relieved glances.

'You should have jumped, Teeny!' Elizabeth told her. 'It was simple. It was silly and dangerous to try to turn back. You'd better not go climbing up trees at all in future.'

The other two juniors were nodding in agreement.

'Shoo away, you two!' Elizabeth said quickly. 'You should be with your tent monitors. Off you go now, and find them! I'll look after Teeny. And don't you go telling the other juniors about this and having them laugh at her. I think we should just pretend it never happened.'

The two children looked at Elizabeth gratefully and scampered off. They had been rather frightened that they might get into trouble, thanks to Teeny being such a coward. But Elizabeth knew that if she were to scold them, it would put them off befriending Teeny another time.

Except, she was not sure that there *would* be another time.

'I think we should give up on Teeny,' she overheard Kitty say.

'But she does like us so,' replied Duncan. 'Shall we just try the . . .'

His voice faded into the distance. It sounded like – '. . . the green ear'.

Elizabeth frowned, puzzled. Whatever was Duncan talking about? Green ear? Try the green ear?

She must have misheard!

Teeny looked so sad as she watched them go. Elizabeth felt sorry for her, in spite of everything. Why did she have to be such a baby and so scared of everything? She was her own worst enemy!

They hurried back and woke Joan, just as Mr Leslie's whistle blew. On the way back to Whyteleafe, Elizabeth whispered to Joan what had happened.

Joan was conscience-stricken.

'I shouldn't have gone to sleep like that! I should have watched the whole time. Oh, thank goodness she wasn't hurt.'

'If she had been, it would have been her own silly fault!' said Elizabeth, crossly. 'Don't fret about Teeny so, Joan. We can forget about it now.'

Unfortunately, it did not prove possible to forget about it.

That evening, Teeny's glasses kept slipping down her nose. She showed them to Arabella, who was in the tent at the time.

'Why, the frames are damaged!' said Arabella knowledgeably. 'Look, there's a little screw missing that should hold the earpiece tight in place. How on earth did that happen?'

'It must have been when I fell out of the

tree,' Teeny responded.

'Tree? What tree?' asked Arabella sharply. 'Where was Joan when this happened?' She proceeded to question Teeny carefully.

Joan was upset to find out about the spectacles. She took them straight to Matron, who was confident that Mr Leslie could mend them by morning. Matron also insisted on handing Joan a lightweight sleeping bag.

'I thought you must have come to collect this, Joan! William said you would probably want to try it out tonight.'

'Oh, I'm *so* pleased you won't have to sleep in the thick one tonight, Joan,' said Arabella, pointedly, when Joan brought it back to the tent. 'It will be so lovely for the rest of us to have the flap closed.'

Joan stared at her, miserably.

A few minutes later, her misery increased tenfold. They were all settled down in their sleeping bags for the night. Patiently,

Arabella waited until Teeny was sound asleep. Then she launched forth.

'I was very shocked to find out how Teeny broke her glasses, Joan,' she whispered indignantly. 'Fancy your just allowing her to run off on her own, like that! Elizabeth tries to cover up for you all the time. But, if you don't mind my saying so, I do think you are turning out to be a hopeless tent monitor!'

Elizabeth ground her teeth in dismay. How very unhelpful of Teeny to be such a coward and to fall and break her glasses! Joan was such a fine tent monitor; she worried about Teeny all the time. How dare Arabella say such things! At the same time, realised Elizabeth, this looked like more trouble for her best friend.

Joan just lay there, rigid, saying nothing.

8 Joan tells Elizabeth the truth

Elizabeth found it difficult to get to sleep. She was too churned up, feeling exasperated with Teeny, furious with Arabella and above all worried about Joan. She lay there for some time, as outside the dusk slowly faded and the tent grew ever darker.

At last, when it was pitch black inside the tent, her eyes began to close . . .

And suddenly were wide open!

Had she dreamed it just now, or had Joan left the tent?

Surely not. The flap was securely tied; the tent was still in pitch darkness.

'Joan?' she whispered.

There was no reply.

She wriggled out of her sleeping bag and crawled across to Joan's. She felt it with her hands. It was empty. So she hadn't dreamed it!

It was strictly forbidden to leave the tent at night without very good reason. Was Joan feeling ill? Elizabeth lay there for a few minutes, waiting for her friend to return. But Joan did not come back.

I must go and look for her! decided Elizabeth, feeling alarmed.

As quietly as possible, she struggled into her dressing gown, then crawled out of the tent. She was very careful all the while not to disturb Arabella. That would be a disaster!

What *was* Joan up to?

It was a warm night outside. There was more cloud cover than last night but with just enough moonlight to see by. Elizabeth gazed around. Where should she begin to look?

She tiptoed round to the back of the tent, glancing this way and that, her ears attuned for the merest sound.

Down in the cutting, where clumps of grass grew beside the empty stream bed, she could hear the whirring of crickets. Then, suddenly, something else –

A tiny, sobbing sound!

She ran up over the top of the bank, then dropped down the other side.

'Joan!' she whispered.

She could see a forlorn figure down there, in a dressing gown, huddled up near the culvert that led beneath the boundary wall. Her shoulders were gently heaving. In some alarm, Elizabeth ran to her and placed an arm round her shoulders.

'Joan, what are you sitting down here for?' she whispered. 'Why ever aren't you in the tent?'

'I can't go back in there!' Joan sobbed quietly. 'I keep trying to pluck up courage but I can't. It's pitch black in there, you see, Elizabeth.'

'Joan, I don't understand—'

'I'm so ashamed,' sobbed Joan. 'I can't bear anyone in the world to know. Not even you, Elizabeth . . .'

But now she blurted out the truth.

'I didn't want the torch batteries for Teeny. I wanted them for my own sake. Then, when I realised none of you wanted the torch on, I lay awake for hours, terrified. That's why I opened the tent flap in the end. Not for Teeny's sake. It was for myself. I just knew I would never sleep if I couldn't have any light in the tent. Elizabeth, I can't get to sleep if its pitch dark. Never, ever!'

'Oh, Joan!' gasped Elizabeth, struggling to take all this in.

Her friend was frightened of the dark! Elizabeth would never have guessed it. How well Joan had kept her secret!

'But, Joan, how can you get to sleep in the dormitory at nights?'

'Because there's always a light in the corridor. The teachers always leave it on for us, don't they? So a nice crack of light comes under the door and that's all I need, Elizabeth. As long as I can see some light, I'm all right.'

'Poor Joan!' whispered Elizabeth. She took her handkerchief out of her dressing gown pocket and dried her friend's eyes for her. 'You mustn't cry. It's not your fault! Can't we explain to somebody about it?'

'How can we?' asked Joan in despair. 'First of all, I can't bear anyone to know. You *must* understand that, Elizabeth. And secondly, they would never let me be tent monitor. How can they allow someone who's frightened of the dark to be in charge of a junior? Especially a nervy little thing like Teeny. The poor child looks up to me so. If she found out about my silly fears, she would be frightened, too. It would put the idea into her head that the dark is something scary when it's not. What sort of example would I be setting?'

At the mention of Teeny's name, Elizabeth felt a moment's annoyance. Oh, no, not Teeny again!

But then, of course, it dawned on her.

She had been blaming Teeny quite unfairly. All the things that had gone wrong so far had not been Teeny's fault, after all. Even the accident with the glasses this afternoon would never have happened if Joan had had a proper night's sleep and been awake enough to look after her!

The root of it all, Elizabeth was forced to admit to herself, was Joan's secret fear. Teeny had not been to blame.

'I'm afraid if we told anybody, there would be only one outcome,' Joan was saying, calmly. In spite of everything, it had given her comfort to confide in Elizabeth at last. 'I would probably be asked to sleep up at school at nights. And Arabella would probably be made tent monitor in my place.'

Elizabeth realised that this was true.

Now, at once, her eyes glinted. She was not going to allow *that* to happen! She had made a solemn vow to help Joan make a success of things. She was not going to let anything defeat her, not even this.

'We've got to think of something, Joan.'

Surely there must be some way round the problem?

She left Joan's side for a moment and peered into the culvert. She crawled inside it for a short distance. She was looking into pitch darkness. The old tunnel ran under the wide country lane that lay beyond the school's boundary wall. It would once have carried the bubbling waters of the stream beneath the road, then out into open farmland on the other side.

'It's lovely and warm, just inside here, Joan!' she said, as she emerged. 'Come down here, a minute!'

'What are you doing, Elizabeth?' asked Joan, coming and crouching down beside her.

Elizabeth was on her knees now, moving rubble and fallen brick away from the entrance to the culvert. She cleared a space, then lay down in a bed of dock leaves, just inside. She was excited.

'I've had a brilliant idea, Joan!' she whispered. 'Let's go and get your sleeping bag from the tent. You can sleep in here! It'll be warm and cosy but you'll still be able to peep out and see the moon and stars above!'

Joan lay down for a moment in the space that Elizabeth had cleared. Suddenly, she looked pleased.

'I really think I could sleep here,

Elizabeth,' she said. 'I really think I would rather like it!'

'Come on, then!' hissed Elizabeth, taking her friend's hand. 'Let's go and get the sleeping bag. You'll need the thick one. And – I know! When you've gone, I'll stuff your kitbag inside the other one! If anyone should chance to look at it in the early morning, they will think it's you lying there, sound asleep.'

'Of course!' said Joan, in delight. 'But I shall be sure to creep back to the tent, as soon as dawn breaks, and be safely back in my place by morning. Oh, Elizabeth. I can do this every night! What a glorious plan.'

'But now we must be as quiet as mice,' whispered Elizabeth, as they crept silently back up the bank. 'If Arabella wakes up, our plan will be ruined.'

Unbeknown to the two friends, Arabella was already awake. She was not only awake but up and about.

She was a light sleeper. The slight draught that had been caused by Elizabeth's leaving the tent had roused her.

Gradually, she had become aware that she and Teeny were alone in the tent. So she had scrambled into her dressing gown and ducked out of the tent herself. Where were the other two? She would try to find out what on earth they thought they were doing!

'I can hear you!' she hissed, in a loud triumphant whisper. She was coming this way. 'I can hear you larking about down there!'

Just below the embankment, the two friends froze like statues. Arabella was coming. She knew they were there!

'I shall have to report this to Miss Ranger!' Arabella was saying.

Joan gazed at Elizabeth in dismay. Arabella had woken up. They were about to be discovered. Oh, what horrible luck!

In her desperation, an idea came to Elizabeth. She whispered it into Joan's ear. This was an emergency. It was the only thing she could think of to do.

It was to be an example of the Naughtiest Girl at her most headstrong.

9 Arabella is made tent monitor

Arms outstretched, like someone in a trance, Elizabeth appeared over the top of the bank. She was moving at speed. She would have crashed straight into Arabella if the other girl had not jumped clear.

Arabella stared in surprise as the figure shot past her in the pale moonlight.

Elizabeth was walking stiffly, her eyes tightly shut, her arms as straight as pokers in front of her. She appeared to be walking in her sleep, marching towards the area where the tents stood.

Joan was following along in her wake.

'Hey, you two—!' began Arabella, as

Joan carried straight on past her. 'What's going on—?'

Joan put a finger to her lips.

'Sssh, Arabella. Sleepwalking! Mustn't be woken up suddenly. Dangerous. Just trying to keep an eye on her . . .'

Elizabeth was playing the part with gusto.

She was striding past Philippa's tent now, her hands still outstretched as though feeling her way. Arabella frowned suspiciously and started to run to catch up with her. She must get a proper look at Elizabeth's face. Was she really asleep? Was it true that she was walking in her sleep? Arabella found it hard to believe *that*.

As Arabella came up alongside her, Elizabeth quickly screwed her eyes shut again. She quickened her pace. It was horrid not to be able to see where she was going! She must get away from Arabella.

She strode on fast and then faster and then . . .

Whoomph! *Crash*!

She tripped over the guy ropes of someone's tent. She hit the guys with such force that the tent pegs came clean out of the ground!

As she fell heavily against the small, green tent there came a horrible creaking, crashing sound –

The smart little tent began to subside. She heard a strangled cry from inside.

'What is going *on*?'

The tent was lying on the ground now. Miss Ranger's angry face appeared from under the folds of limp canvas.

Elizabeth could only sit there and stare in horror. She had brought the teacher's tent down on top of her while she slept!

Miss Ranger struggled out from beneath the fallen tent, found her dressing gown and slipped it on over her pyjamas. She confronted Elizabeth, who had now got to her feet and been joined by both Joan and Arabella.

'What exactly is the meaning of this tomfoolery, Elizabeth?' she asked. 'What are you all doing out of your tent, may I ask?'

'I think Elizabeth may have been sleepwalking—' Joan began, desperately.

'You fibber!' exclaimed Arabella. 'Elizabeth was only pretending. And you were only pretending to be looking after her! You just did it because I'd come to see where you were! I heard you talking together before that. I heard you larking around!'

'Are you saying, Arabella, that Joan and Elizabeth were out of the tent at night?' asked Miss Ranger. 'And that you had to go and look for them?'

'Yes, Miss Ranger. And Elizabeth *can't* have been sleepwalking!' Arabella continued, triumphantly. 'Look, she's wearing her dressing gown! Whoever heard of someone remembering to put on their dressing gown before they start walking in their sleep?'

The teacher had only to look at the two guilty faces to know that Arabella was speaking the truth.

'I can see that camping has gone to Elizabeth's head,' observed Miss Ranger. 'I thought she was much more sensible these days. But I am shocked at *your* behaviour, Joan. That you, a tent monitor, should have been joining in Elizabeth's pranks! I am beginning to wonder if I did the right thing to put you in charge of Teeny Wilson.'

'Joan let Teeny go off and climb a tree in the woods this afternoon!' Arabella blurted out. 'And Teeny fell out of the tree and broke her glasses!'

Miss Ranger was taken aback. Telling tales was not encouraged at Whyteleafe

School. But, occasionally, the teachers agreed, it could be justified.

'Is this true, Joan?' she asked.

Joan stared at the ground and said nothing. She was deeply mortified.

'It was only a low branch she fell off!' Elizabeth protested. 'And she didn't hurt herself at all.'

'Thank you, Elizabeth, that will do,' replied the teacher. 'I can see that what Arabella says *is* true, then.'

Miss Ranger gazed at all three girls, wondering what was the correct thing to do. To give herself time to calm down, she asked them to help her right the tent.

Only when that was done did she speak again. The teacher had come to a decision.

'The three of you will now return to your tent, in silence,' she said. 'I shall ask William and Rita to call a Special Meeting for tomorrow afternoon, so that it can be decided whether Joan should remain as a tent monitor, or not.'

Miss Ranger then placed a hand on Arabella's shoulder.

'Until the Special Meeting takes place I appoint you, Arabella, to be acting tent monitor. Until then, you are in charge of the tent and, in particular, I expect you to take good care of Teeny. Do you think you can rise to the challenge, Arabella?'

'Oh, Miss Ranger,' simpered Arabella, longing to gloat but somehow managing to look humble, 'I'll try my very best not to let you down.'

Joan's face was ashen.

And Elizabeth could have screamed with rage.

Elizabeth went to sleep feeling very sorry for herself. It was bad enough that Arabella had been appointed acting tent monitor. But she felt angry, too, at being in disgrace. She dreaded the Special Meeting. She had not set out to be naughty, not at all. Everything she had done had been to help her friend. From the moment she had taken the blame for their being late back from the village ... It had all been for Joan's sake! She had wanted nothing more than for Joan to make the grade as a fine tent monitor. And it had all been in vain, after all.

And now Arabella would tell everyone at the Meeting about the sleepwalking episode! She would be teased and laughed at and called the Naughtiest Girl again ...

But then, shortly before daybreak, Elizabeth was awoken by Arabella's voice.

'I know perfectly well you've got your torch on, inside that sleeping bag, Joan. I can see the light from here. As tent monitor, I must ask you to put it out, please.'

At once, a lump came to her throat.

Poor Joan! Her troubles were so much worse than Elizabeth's own. It seemed that she had managed to snatch a few hours' sleep only by keeping her torch on inside her sleeping bag. Elizabeth heard the torch click off and its feeble light was extinguished.

She longed to protest but she knew that Joan would not thank her for it. How she would hate it if Arabella, of all people, knew about her fear. It would make her more superior than ever!

If only there were some way of *curing* Joan's fear, thought Elizabeth. Suddenly, she dimly remembered staying at a cousin's house. He always had to have the light on at night. 'He will grow out of it,' she had heard her Aunt say to someone. 'The doctor says when he is about ten or eleven.' Why, in that case, Joan should be growing out of her fear any moment now! decided Elizabeth, hopefully. How wonderful if that happened and they could enjoy the rest of camp!

But how *could* they enjoy the rest of camp, she realised dully, with Joan suspended as a tent monitor and the insufferable Arabella appointed in her place? That, surely, was the only possible outcome of this afternoon's Special Meeting.

At that moment, the first twittering of birdsong rose up outside. The dawn chorus was beginning. Soon, the pitch dark inside the tent was giving way to a softer gloom. Comforted by the thought that Joan would now be able to sleep, Elizabeth turned over and went back to sleep herself.

When she awoke, the sun was well up and the tent flap tied back.

Joan was outside somewhere.

Arabella and Teeny were up and dressed. Teeny was kneeling in the centre of the tent, in front of the mirror. Arabella was brushing her hair for her.

'Fifty strokes, morning and night,

make your hair shine, Teeny,' Arabella was saying. 'It will make it shine like mine does!'

The little girl's spectacles had already been returned by Matron and were secure on her nose once more. Drowsily watching Teeny, Elizabeth noticed that she seemed to be preening herself in the mirror. She had buttoned her blue shirt up to the neck and had turned the collar up. She was staring at the image, dreamily, as though she liked it.

Arabella's going to make Teeny as vain as she is herself, thought Elizabeth, as the child fiddled with the shirt, unbuttoned it and turned the collar down again. Now she was asking Arabella why Joan was no longer in charge of her.

'Because Miss Ranger thinks I will make a better job of looking after you,' said Arabella, proudly. 'You'll hear all about it this afternoon. There's going to be a Special Meeting.'

'Oh,' replied Teeny, looking disappointed.

But Arabella did not make a better job of looking after Teeny. She made a very bad job of it. That morning she forgot all about her and the consequences could not have been more dramatic.

10   *Teeny in danger*

'Where's Teeny?' asked Arabella, tetchily. 'I'm waiting to take her for a shower.'

Elizabeth and Joan stared at her in surprise. It was now noon. The two friends had spent the morning at the stables, helping Robert to groom the horses. After that they had been for a short ride. Now, as they returned to their tent, they found Arabella waiting impatiently outside. She was wearing a different outfit from the one she had worn at breakfast.

'How should we know?' asked Elizabeth rudely. It was a relief not to have to be polite to Arabella any more. 'You're the important tent monitor in charge of everything. You should know where Teeny is, not us.'

'But I thought she must have spent the morning with you!' said Arabella. 'When did you last see her?'

'We haven't seen her since breakfast time,' replied Joan, with a puzzled frown. What was this all about? 'You and she were washing up your breakfast things together.'

Both friends had noticed how forlorn the little girl looked this morning. She had not seemed to be enjoying Arabella's company very much. She had been gazing wistfully at Duncan and Kitty. Once again, the two boisterous juniors had been taking no notice of her. Elizabeth had commented to Joan how tragic it was that Teeny had been too cowardly to jump off that branch, the day before.

'How different things might have been!' Elizabeth had sighed. 'For all of us.'

'You mustn't call Teeny a coward,' Joan

had replied, gently. 'We all have things that we're scared of.'

Now, a pallor was creeping over Arabella's face.

'Where is she, then?'

'Do you mean to say you haven't seen her all morning, either?' asked Elizabeth, accusingly. 'But where have you been? You were supposed to be in charge of her!'

'I had important things to do . . .' began Arabella, lamely. 'She was in the tent when I left her. I didn't mean to be gone very long . . .' Arabella pouted. 'In any case, Teeny said she had something *she* wanted to do.'

'What?' asked Joan, tensely.

'I've no idea,' said Arabella. She clammed up.

The truth was that Arabella had quickly become bored with Teeny's company. After breakfast, she had decided to slip up to school, taking some of her clothes back to exchange for others. She felt that she had brought the wrong outfits to camp and that she would look better in some others.

She had been only too happy when Teeny declined to come with her, saying that she had something of her own to do. And she had left the little girl sitting cross-legged in the tent, shuffling those silly playing cards, lost in thought.

Once in her dormitory, Arabella had soon forgotten about Teeny altogether. Admiring herself in a wardrobe mirror, she had tried on outfit after outfit and quite lost track of time. She had only just returned to the tent.

'You had better start looking for her,' said Elizabeth grimly. 'Hadn't you, Arabella?'

'Elizabeth and I will run to Camp Centre and see if she's there,' said Joan, anxiously. 'If we can't find her quickly, we must tell Miss Ranger.'

Leaving the frightened Arabella peering, helplessly, into empty tents, the friends raced off.

When they reached Camp Centre, they dearly hoped to find Teeny there. Had the loneliness of being left on her own all morning made her force herself to come and mix with her classmates? Perhaps they would find her playing happily with some other juniors, at last.

But there was no sign of her.

Most children had already left with their tent monitors to have a shower before dinner. Duncan and Kitty were loitering about and chatting happily to two of their classmates. That was all.

'Have you seen Teeny, any of you?' asked Joan softly, as she and Elizabeth walked up. 'Arabella's waiting to take her for a shower.'

Joan spoke in a calm, quiet voice for she did not want to alarm the younger children in any way.

'Not since breakfast,' volunteered Kitty.

'We've been helping Mr Leslie build some plate racks this morning,' said Duncan. He pointed proudly into the Kitchen Area. A row of plate racks stood there, made from green twigs criss-crossed and lashed together. 'Now we won't have to do so much drying up. We can leave things to dry in the sun, Mr Leslie says. Do you like them?'

'Yes, very good,' said Joan, absently, at the same time gazing everywhere for some sign of Teeny. 'Well done.'

Elizabeth, however, was staring at the children in fascination.

All four had their sports shirts buttoned up to the neck and the collars turned up. It was the new fashion amongst some of the juniors, as Elizabeth was already vaguely aware. But today they also wore what looked like a fat sprig of grass tucked in behind the top button. It was worn discreetly, almost like a secret badge.

Then some tent monitors appeared in the distance, shouting to the juniors to come up to school with them for their showers.

'Well,' said Joan worriedly, as the four juniors went racing off, 'Teeny can't have been at Camp Centre all morning, or those four would have seen her. Oh, Elizabeth, it was very wrong of Arabella not to find out what it was Teeny wanted to do. If only we knew that, it would be much easier to find her.'

Elizabeth was thinking hard. A picture flashed into her mind of Teeny this morning – of her turning her collar up, admiring herself in the mirror.

'I thought the juniors' shirts were just some kind of fashion,' she told Joan excitedly. 'But now I'm not so sure. I think it might be some kind of club – and that

Teeny wants to join it. And maybe being asked to jump from the branch yesterday was somehow connected with it—'

She stared at her friend.

'Joan, do you think she might have gone back there this morning? To try the jump again? On her own?'

'Why would she do that?'

'Well, hoping to be let into the club . . .?' mused Elizabeth.

'If you're right, we'd better go and tell Miss Ranger straight away,' said Joan. 'But why should the juniors have a club? You know they get crazes about how to wear things . . .'

'But the stems of grass they were wearing!' replied Elizabeth. 'It was those as well. They could be some kind of badge!'

'Grass?' asked Joan. 'Oh, you mean those green ears of corn? I noticed them wearing them last night, round the camp fire.'

Elizabeth gasped.

Green ears of corn. Of course!

Excitedly she told Joan what she had overheard Duncan say to Kitty in the woods yesterday. About Teeny.

But she does like us so. Shall we just try the green ear . . .

Joan now became very interested.

'So you think Duncan and Kitty are the club leaders and they decided to give Teeny another chance? They told her last night that she could go and get a green ear of corn, like theirs . . .? And *that's* where she's gone to this morning?'

'I'm sure of it!' exclaimed Elizabeth. 'But I'm sure they don't know about it. Teeny's made up her mind this morning, all on her own, to try and do it. To prove she's not a coward. That means it must be somewhere quite difficult . . .'

'But where?' asked Joan. 'Oh, we must *think* . . .'

The whole camp had been to the woods yesterday. But there was certainly no corn growing there. Nor had they passed any on the way back. And, of course, there was no corn growing anywhere in the school grounds.

Yet at no time were members of the junior class permitted to go out of the school grounds on their own. So how had they managed to get those fresh-looking ears of corn?

'The only place I've ever seen any corn growing is over there somewhere,' said Elizabeth. 'On the other side of the lane.'

She waved a hand vaguely in the direction they had just come from. Out riding last July, she had seen a huge field of golden corn and men getting the harvest in. At the moment, of course, it would still be green. The field, she now realised, must lie opposite the high wall where their tent was pitched.

She gasped.

'I think I know how they did it!'

Joan had realised the same thing.

The two friends raced to the footbridge and swung themselves down into the dried-up stream bed. They ran all the way along the cutting, puffing and panting, until the mouth of the culvert came in sight.

'Listen!' cried Joan, as they neared its entrance.

From deep in the darkness came a faint whimpering sound.

Teeny was trapped somewhere in the tiny tunnel!

Remembering the pitch blackness in there, Joan hesitated. Only one of them would be able to squeeze in. But Teeny was in there. There was not a second to lose!

She wanted to do it. She had been Teeny's tent monitor. She *must* do it. But she knew that Elizabeth would stop her. And that would be more than enough to make her nerve fail . . .

Elizabeth glanced at her friend's face and saw everything that was going through her mind.

She ran forward, tripped and fell to the ground. She gave a cry.

'My ankle! I think I've done something!'

Now Joan could hesitate no longer.

'It's all right, Elizabeth. Don't try to move! I'm going in there to get Teeny!'

Joan dropped to the ground, dived through the gap, then crawled forward into the darkness and was gone.

Soon Elizabeth heard her voice, echoing from deep inside the culvert.

'It's all right, Teeny. It's Joan here. Don't be frightened. We'll get you out of here!'

Elizabeth got to her feet and tiptoed forward. There was nothing wrong with her ankle, at all.

Peering into the blackness, she could

hear the clunk of rubble being moved. The roof of the culvert must have collapsed. Joan must be clearing a path for Teeny, with her bare hands. The child had been overcome with panic. She had lain there, not daring to move, convinced that she was trapped.

The little tunnel, like an echo chamber, carried their voices out.

'We'll just move these last few bricks, Teeny, and there'll be a nice gap and I'll be able to pull you through. We must do everything very slowly and carefully, so that we don't make any more disturbance.'

'Yes, Joan. Oh, Joan, I've been so scared.'

Only Elizabeth knew just how scared *Joan* must be and how brave she was being. Feeling immensely proud of her friend, she raced away to find Miss Ranger and Mr Leslie.

When she returned with the teachers and

with Rita as well, they were just in time to see Joan's rear view appearing. Crawling backwards, Joan was gently pulling Teeny by the hands, out of the culvert, into the fresh air.

'We didn't feel there was any time to waste!' Elizabeth explained to Miss Ranger. 'We were both so frightened Teeny might suffocate.'

'I think the whole school is going to be very proud of Joan,' replied the teacher. 'She can take great pride in what she's done.'

'I think she does already,' replied Elizabeth, looking at Joan's happy, glowing face as she hugged Teeny close.

Teeny, in spite of her frightening ordeal, was also looking very proud. Her tearstained face was, just like Joan's, glowing with happiness and a sense of achievement.

There was something clutched in her

grimy fingers. She held it up to show Joan.

'Look! Duncan and Kitty will be friends with me now!' she blurted out. 'I shall be allowed to be a member of the Dare Club.'

It was a green ear of corn.

11   A very good school meeting

The Special Meeting was about to begin.
The campers sat on the ground sheets in
rows, again. A low buzz of conversation
rippled up and down the rows. It was
always very exciting and interesting when
William and Rita called a Special Meeting.
It meant that there was something
important to discuss.

Sitting with her classmates, Elizabeth
wondered what exactly was going to be
raised at the Meeting.

It was no longer going to be about who
should be tent monitor between Joan and
Arabella.

There was Joan, at the front, seated with

the other tent monitors. Elizabeth smiled and waved to her friend. Proudly, Joan waved back. She was back in her rightful place.

As soon as Teeny's rescue had taken place, Miss Ranger had stripped Arabella of her acting monitorship and asked Joan to resume her duties. Arabella was in deep disgrace for neglecting the little junior in her charge when it was well known that Teeny had no little friends to play with.

But Teeny certainly had friends now! thought Elizabeth, with a smile.

It had been wonderful to watch her at lunch time, surrounded by the other members of the Dare Club. In clean clothes, after a hot shower, she had sat between Duncan and Kitty, in the place of honour at one of the junior tables. She was a member of the club at last, her collar worn turned up, like the rest of them, her green ear of corn displayed like a trophy in her top buttonhole. Having no idea of the danger she had been through, Duncan and Kitty were simply pleased that Teeny had finally proved that she was not a 'coward'.

She was still sitting with her new friends now, chattering happily in the front row, a child transformed.

Since arriving at Whyteleafe, the shy, nervous girl had longed only to be friends with Duncan and Kitty – she liked and admired them so. They had promised her that once she had proved her courage with a successful 'Dare', she would be allowed to join their secret club and play with them.

But each time Teeny had been given a Dare to do, her courage had failed and she had not completed it. With each failure, her confidence had ebbed away. The more desperate she became to join the club, the more scared and jumpy she was; dreading each new Dare, yet longing to succeed. Her greatest battle had been with herself. This morning, sitting in the tent and struggling with her fears, she knew that the challenge, to crawl through the culvert and pick a green ear of corn in the field that was out of bounds, was her very last chance. Duncan and Kitty would not give her another. And she had won the battle!

'Silence, please!' called William, banging the mallet on the table. 'At the Meeting this afternoon, we are going to talk about courage.'

There was an immediate hush.

Rita then told the astonished Meeting about the fall of rubble in the dangerous old tunnel. She told how it was only thanks to the alertness of Elizabeth and the bravery of Joan that no harm had befallen Teeny Wilson.

The two friends stood up and were given a round of applause.

Then William took over.

'We believe that Teeny's narrow escape

had something to do with a Dare,' he said. 'If so, would the person or persons who made the Dare please stand up?'

Sitting in the front row, Duncan and Kitty had turned pale. They exchanged frightened glances but remained sitting.

'Would they please stand and own up?' William repeated.

The two juniors sat very, very still. They were frozen with fear.

William sighed.

'In that case—' He banged the mallet sharply on the table, making everyone jump. 'Duncan and Kitty, I must ask you to stand up at once and come out here to the front.'

Trembling slightly, the little boy and girl got slowly to their feet and went and stood in the front. Their faces had turned red with shame.

'I see,' said William. He surveyed them. 'How very interesting. So even you two are frightened of something? You are frightened of Rita and I.'

Now Rita joined in.

'William and I have made a full investigation. We have discovered, though not from Teeny, that all term you have been calling her a coward. You have been setting her Dares to do that were beyond her capabilities. In doing so, all her confidence was destroyed. You did not mean it to be cruel. You wanted her to succeed. But cruel it was.'

Duncan and Kitty, and some other members of the Dare Club, too, were beginning to feel extremely uncomfortable. Teeny's mouth was hanging open, in wonder, that the head-boy and girl had found all this out.

From the rest of the campers, there came not a sound.

As William continued, they hung on to every word he said.

'What you must all learn and understand,' he said, 'is that there are many different forms of courage and many different forms of cowardice. Let me give you an example. One Dare you set Teeny, when we all got to camp, was to play a joke on someone in her tent. Because she was discovered, you told Teeny that she had failed. But do you know why she was discovered?'

Kitty and Duncan shook their heads.

'She was discovered because *another* girl was blamed. So what did Teeny do? Rather than let the other girl take the blame, she owned up. Did that not take courage?'

Slowly, the juniors nodded.

'And *not* to have owned up – would that not have been cowardly?' prompted Rita. 'And should you not have owned up just now, when William asked you to?'

'So who are the real cowards, you or Teeny?' concluded William.

'We are,' said Duncan, looking deeply ashamed.

The lesson had been well and truly learned. Rita spoke to them now, almost gently.

'It is not brave or clever to make sleeping-bag jokes, or to break school rules, or do dangerous things. It must stop. But we want you all to put this behind you now and enjoy the rest of camp. And I think the monitors have decided that you must give your club a new name. Can any of you think of one?'

'Let's call it the Friendship Club!' exclaimed Kitty, taking hold of Teeny's hand. 'Would that be a good name, Teeny? Do you like it?'

Teeny loved it. They all did.

Afterwards, the whole camp agreed that it had been a very good Meeting. They had all learned something from it, including Elizabeth.

'In a way, I'm as bad as those little juniors,' she confessed to Joan later, as they sunned themselves outside the tent. 'I thought Teeny was a terrible coward when she wouldn't jump off that low branch.'

'Yes, William and Rita were so right,' agreed Joan. 'There are so many different ways of being cowardly – and of being brave.'

'And still no-one knows how brave *you* were, Joan,' said Elizabeth. 'Going into that pitch black tunnel. It would have meant nothing to me. But for you, of all people—'

'And nobody is going to know, either!' replied Joan, quickly. 'It was a private battle and I know now that I have won it. I am going to sleep without any light in the tent tonight, Elizabeth! You wait and see!'

Then she turned to her friend.

'It was so lucky that you fell, at exactly the right moment. I don't think I would have had the courage to go on, if that hadn't happened. I was convinced you must have twisted your ankle. Are you sure that it's really better now?'

'It seems absolutely fine,' replied Elizabeth solemnly. She bent forward, as though to examine it. In fact, she was making sure that Joan would not see the smile on her face.

After such a bad start, camp turned out to be wonderful. There was no more trouble with Arabella, certainly none with Teeny and, true to her word, Joan found that she could manage the darkness after that. Everyone was to agree that Joan turned out to be a very fine tent monitor, just as Elizabeth had vowed that they would.

Joan wanted to tell Miss Ranger that, for private reasons, she – Joan – was to blame for the visit to the village and for the sleepwalking episode. But

Elizabeth refused to allow her.

'It would all be too complicated,' she said, with a shrug. 'And besides, the sleepwalking was such a terrible idea. I would rather we all forgot about it.'

It had not been one of the Naughtiest Girl's best. The last one, the falling over idea, had been much better. Elizabeth was pleased about that. She could bear one or two black marks against her name, just to see her best friend happy again.

Elizabeth was not without courage herself.

About the Author

Anne Digby was born in Kingston upon Thames and is married with one one and three daughters. As a child she loved reading and the first full length book she ever read on her own (and her first introduction to Enid Blyton) was the Blyton translation of Jean de Brunoff's *The Story of Babar, the Little Elephant*, from the French. From there it was a short step to enjoying Enid Blyton's own adventure stories of which her favourite was *The Secret Mountain*. Anne has now had over thirty children's novels published of her own, including the *Trebizon* school series and the *Me, Jill Robinson* series of family adventures and has been translated into many languages. This is her second book in the *Enid Blyton's Naughtiest Girl* series, the rest of which are listed below.

THE NAUGHTIEST GIRL KEEPS A SECRET
Elizabeth intends never to be naughty again. But then John entrusts her with his secret . . .

THE NAUGHTIEST GIRL SAVES THE DAY
Elizabeth longs to star in the school summer play, but she will have to behave. So why make a hoax fire alarm? wonders Julian . . .

WELL DONE, THE NAUGHTIEST GIRL!
The worst girl in the school – or the best? It's the end of the school year and Elizabeth's fate will soon be decided!